Disney's Lilo & Stitch

Say Cheese!

Illustrated by Caroline Egan and the Disney Storybook Artists
Designed by Disney's Global Design Group

Random House New York
A Random House PICTUREBACK® Shape Book

Library of Congress Control Number: 2001093821
ISBN: 0-7364-1323-5
www.randomhouse.com/kids/disney
Printed in the United States of America May 2002
10 9 8 7 6 5 4 3 2 1

Hi. I'm Lilo.

This is a picture my sister, Nani, took of me.

This is a picture I drew of Nani.

I love to take pictures.
This is Pudge the fish.

He controls the weather.

I live in Hawaii, where it's warm and sunny almost every day!

This is my house.

I ❤ HAWAII

Uh-oh! Here's Nani trying to make dinner.

She's not the world's greatest cook!

Surf Sandwich Shoppe

For the best subs in town!

555-HERO

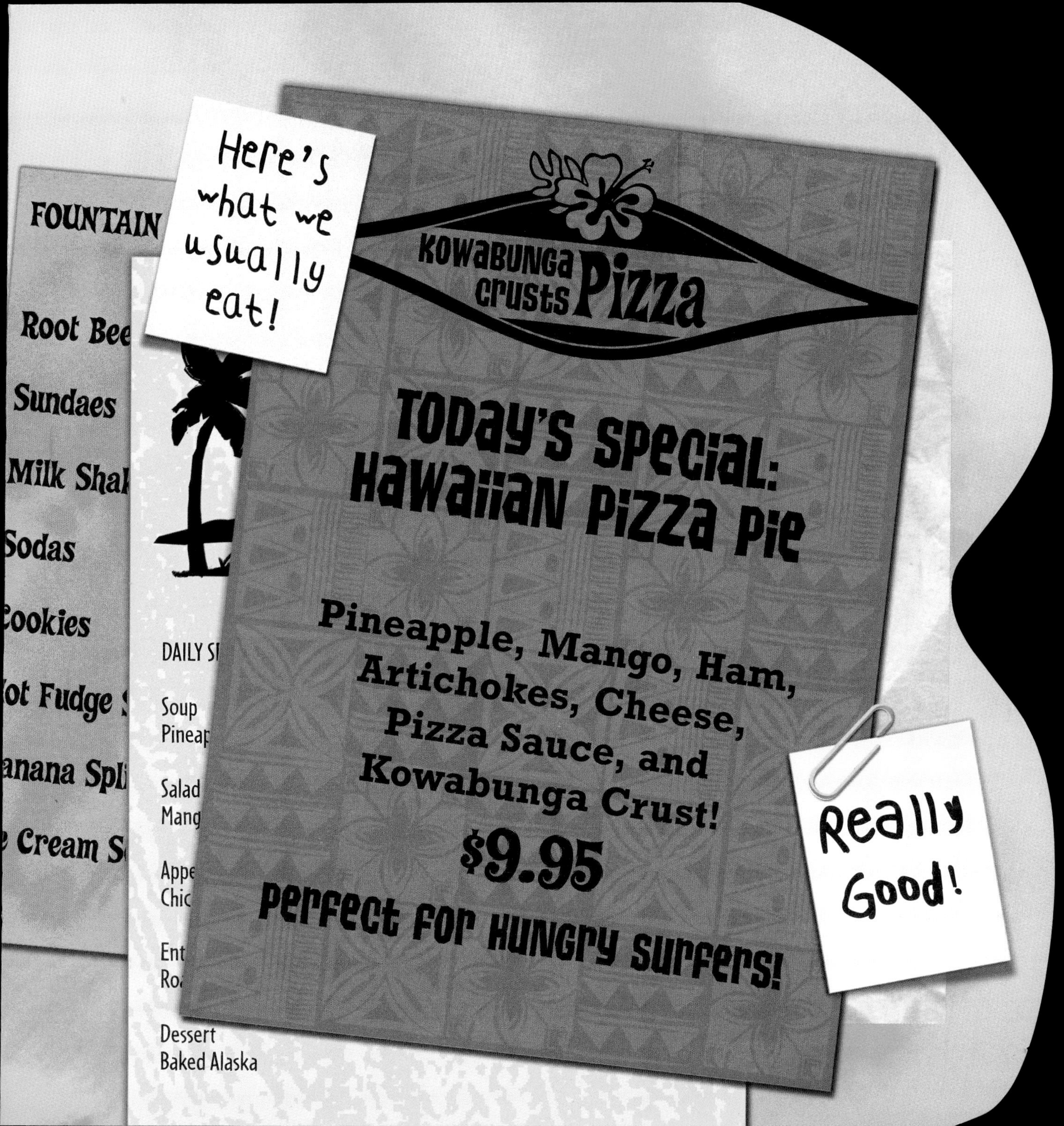
Here's what we usually eat!
FOUNTAIN
Root Bee
Sundaes
Milk Shak
Sodas
ookies
ot Fudge
anana Spli
Cream S
DAILY S
Soup
Pineap
Salad
Mang
Appe
Chic
Ent
Ro
Dessert
Baked Alaska
KOWABUNGA crusts Pizza
TODAY'S SPECIAL: HAWAIIAN PIZZA PIE
Pineapple, Mango, Ham, Artichokes, Cheese, Pizza Sauce, and Kowabunga Crust!
$9.95
PERFECT FOR HUNGRY SURFERS!
Really Good!

This is Cobra Bubbles. He's my social worker.

Marion "Cobra" Bubbles, M.A.

Domestic Security Supervisor,
Level 27

The one you call when things go wrong.
555-COBRA

He looks mean, but he's actually very nice!

I love to hula dance.

I am an excellent hula dancer!

This is my hula lamp.

This is my hula teacher.

Here are my friends.
I think they've got issues.

This is Myrtle in the middle. She has the most issues of all!

This is me and my doll, Scrump.
I made her myself.

Here's what I used to make her:
Beans
Green Sock
Red Yarn
Yellow Pipe cleaners
Pink Bow
3 different buttons
Isn't she cute?

Here are some more pictures of me.

This is David.

He has fancy hair.

This is my dog, Stitch.
He's not like other dogs.

Stitch's badness level is very high sometimes.

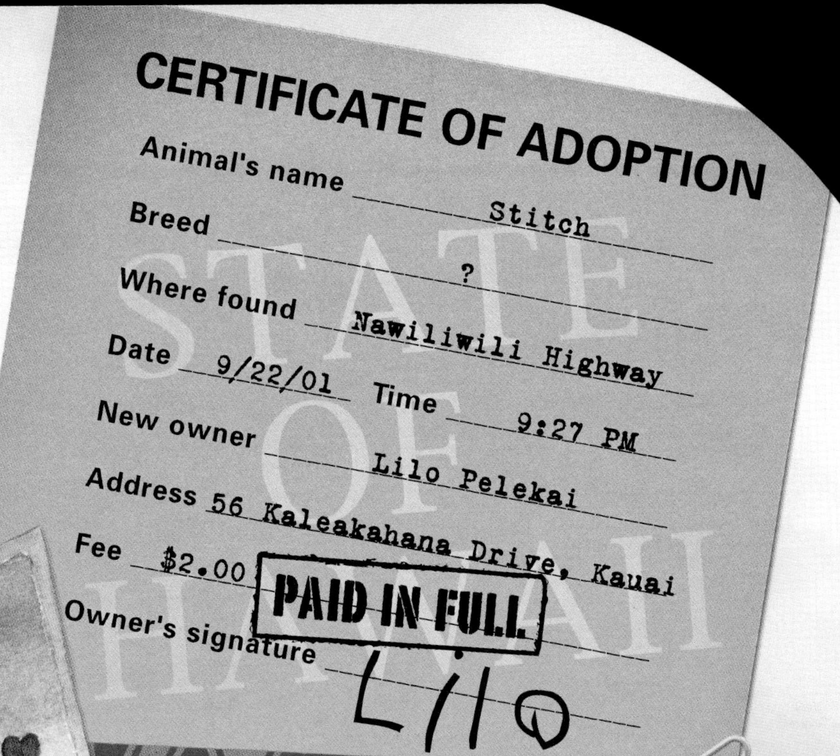

CERTIFICATE OF ADOPTION

STATE OF HAWAII

Animal's name Stitch

Breed ?

Where found Nawiliwili Highway

Date 9/22/01 Time 9:27 PM

New owner Lilo Pelekai

Address 56 Kaleakahana Drive, Kauai

Fee $2.00

PAID IN FULL

Owner's signature Lilo

That's my dog!

Have you ever seen a dog do a headstand?

Stitch's Tricks

1. Builds sand castles
2. Operates blender
3. Rides a trike really fast
4. Plays the ukulele
5. Does laundry

Or read?

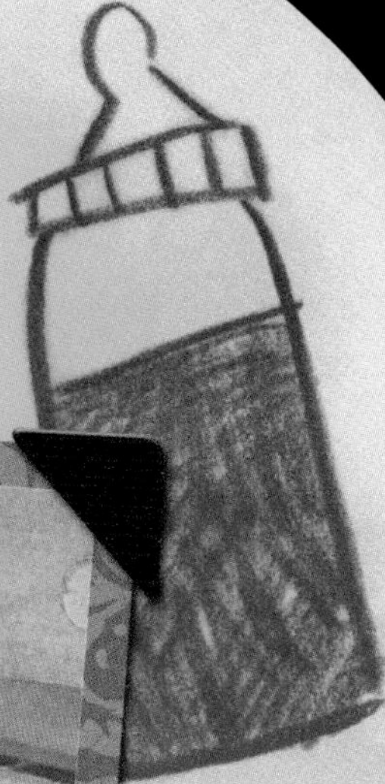

He's the smartest dog ever!

Or cook dinner?

Super Stitch!

I love the beach. There are so many interesting things to see.

Stitch has left the building.

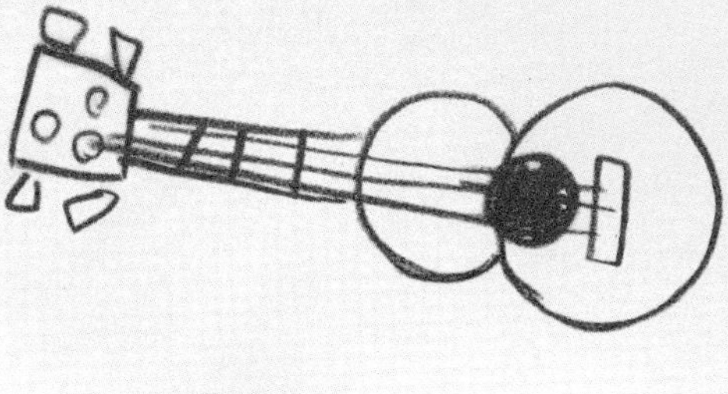

Action shot!

Stitch likes to surf almost as much as I do!

Surf's up!

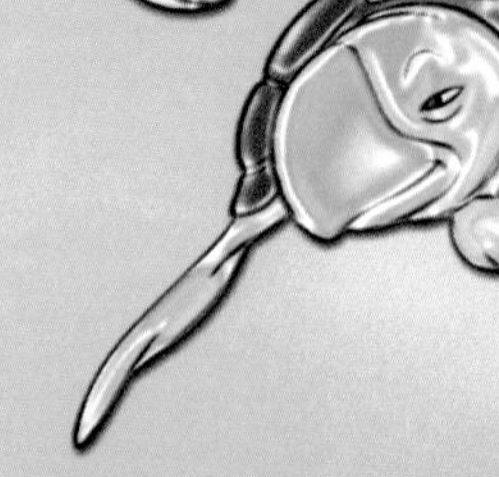

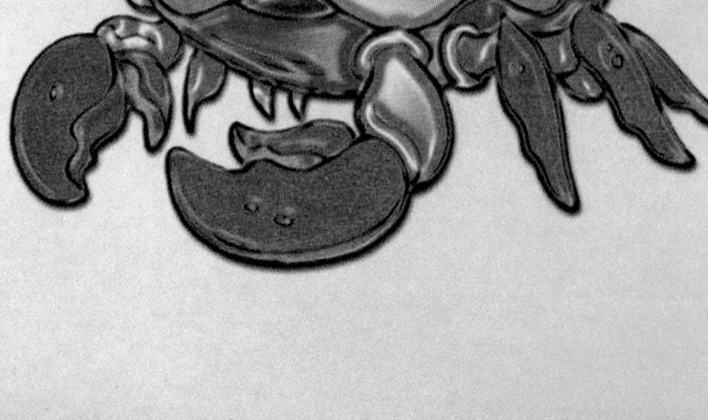

Stitch loves to play around at the beach.

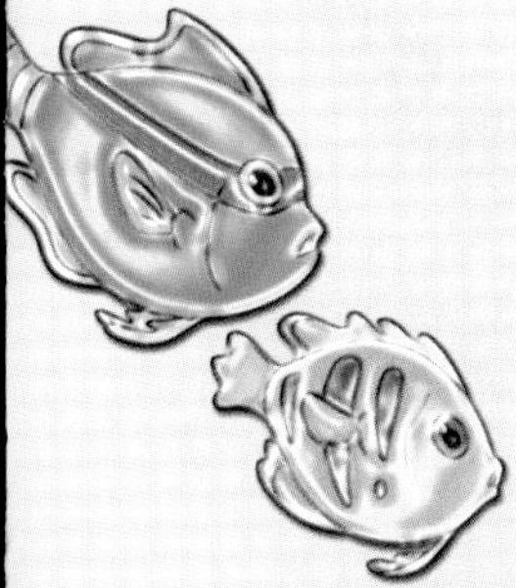

Silly Stitch!

There are lots of tourists in Hawaii.

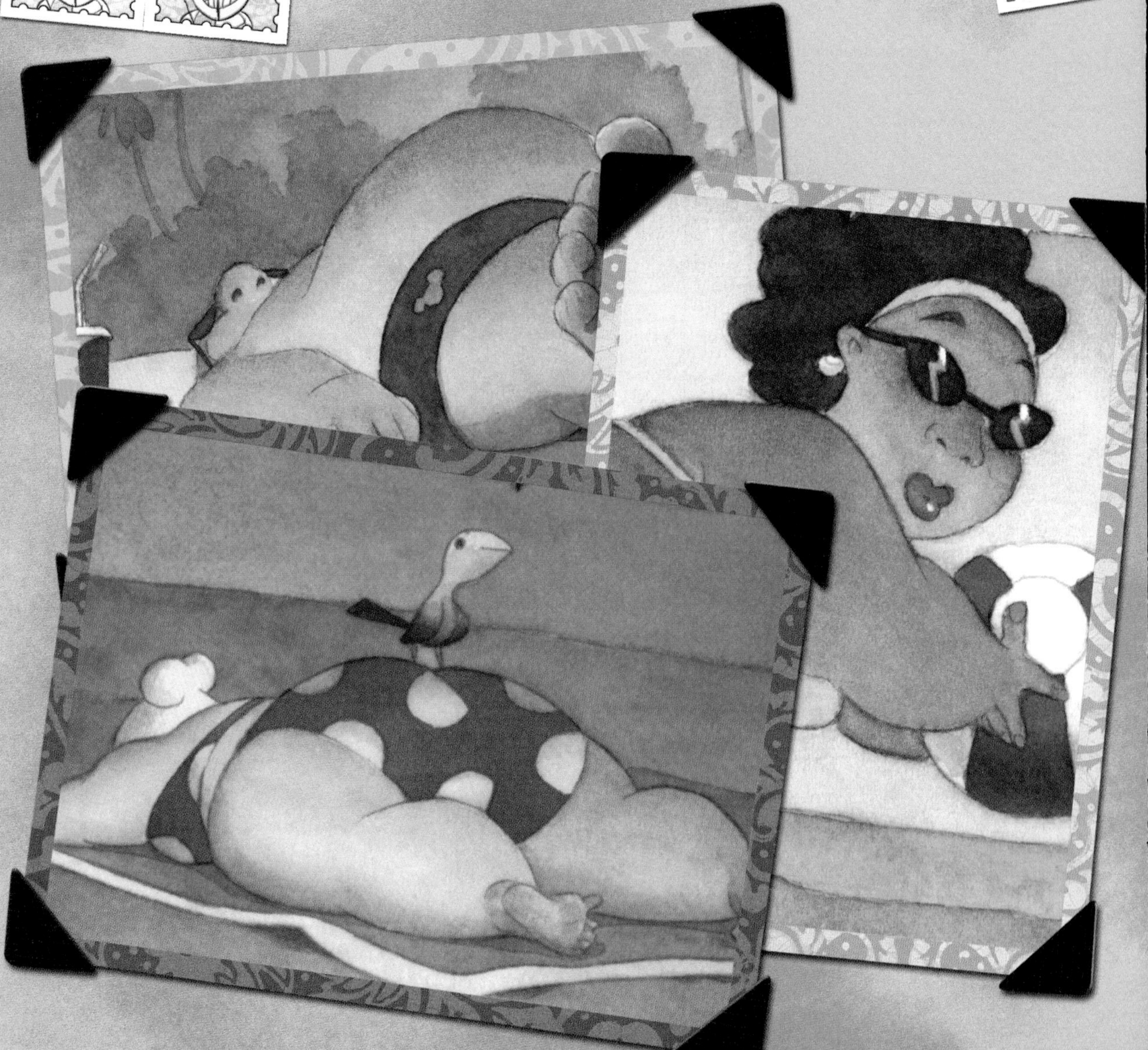

These two are *definitely* the weirdest ones I've ever seen!

Stitch and I have promised to be best friends forever!

Lilo & Stitch